THE WAITING ROOM READER

Stories to Keep You Company

Co-sponsored by CavanKerry Press Ltd.
and The Arnold P. Gold Foundation for Humanism in Medicine

The Arnold P. Gold Foundation

CavanKerry ◆ Press LTD.

CavanKerry Press Ltd.
Fort Lee, New Jersey
www.cavankerrypress.org

Library of Congress Cataloging-in-Publication Data

The waiting room reader : stories to keep you company / editor,
Joan Cusack Handler. — 1st ed.
p. cm.
ISBN-13: 978-1-933880-13-6
ISBN-10: 1-933880-13-9
1. American poetry—21st century. I. Handler, Joan Cusack, 1941- II.
Title.

PS617.W35 2008
811'.608—dc22

2008045247

Cover and interior art by Nancy Stahl © 2008,
Cover and book design by Peter Cusack

First Edition 2009, Printed in the United States of America

Acknowledgements

CavanKerry Press is grateful for the invaluable contribution of:

The Liana Foundation without whose support, *The Reader* would not have been possible

The Arnold P. Gold Foundation for Humanism in Medicine, co-sponsor of our *LaurelBooks: Literature of Illness and Disability* imprint and co-sponsor and distributor of *The Reader*

The writers whose poems are printed here

The Waiting Room Reader Committee responsible for producing the book and bringing it to its readers: designer, editors, administrator and distributors

Editor: Joan Cusack Handler
Designer: Peter Cusack
Editorial Committee: Florenz Eisman, Sandra O. Gold Ed.D.,
                     Susan Jackson, Barbara Packer, Carol Snyder
Distribution: The Gold Foundation- Sandra O. Gold Ed.D.
CKP Administrator: Donna Rutkowski

www.cavankerrypress.org
www.humanism-in-medicine.org

CavanKerry Press is grateful for the
support it receives from the
New Jersey State Council on the Arts.

Dear Patients, Dear Friends,

We're delighted to bring you *The Waiting Room Reader: Stories to Keep You Company.*

The Reader was a long-time dream until this past year when CavanKerry and the Liana and Gold Foundations came together to give it life.

Like you, we too have been patients in waiting rooms of doctors' offices and hospitals. Sometimes for routine care; other times for critical care. We too have waited for x-rays or our annual physical. We too have undergone surgeries and waited long hours alone while a loved one—somewhere beyond our reach—drifted in and out of surgery induced sleep. In all cases, the wait seemed endless. We've needed patience; we've needed laughter; sometimes we've needed hope. We've wished we had company. We thought you might need these too.

In that spirit, we have gathered here a collection of stories and thoughts from CavanKerry writers that focus on life's gifts, everyday gifts and experiences—love and family, food and home, work and play, dreams and the earth. Each piece is short—a page or two at most, some a few lines—and can be read in any order. So start anyplace; read one, read two, read them all. Hopefully, your wait will seem shorter.

All the best,
Joan Cusack Handler
Publisher, Editor
CavanKerry Press Ltd.

Note

We'd love to hear from you. We've added a few blank pages at the
back of *The Reader* for you to record your own stories and share
them with the next reader. Hopefully, you will start a patient
dialogue. Consider sending us a copy. Write or e-mail us and
share your thoughts about *The Reader*. You are the reader we
are trying to reach.

joan@cavankerrypress.org
www.cavankerrypress.org

sgold@gold-foundation.org
www.humanism-in-medicine.org

Contents

My Life, My Self

Everyday Miracles

The Earth

Waiting

We wait for babies to be born, for test results to come back, for phone calls, jobs; we wait beside beds where people lay dying; we wait for love. Today I am waiting on the top of a mountain for the sun to rise. I shiver as wind bites through the crowd huddled together looking east. An old monk chanting prayers reminds me of the ancient people who once called the great sun to come back from where it hides in the night.

I can barely see the barren landscape around me, barely remember how I got here. There was the waking knock on the door at two a.m. I slipped on my clothes, filled my jacket pockets with what might be needed for the climb, then joined the others of our group on the monastery's guest house terrace. We set off, giving ourselves to the big bowl of darkness, to the stars and the small path shone by the light of our own flashlights.

As we pass through the monastery gates we're almost at once in the river of other travelers. The trail of hikers and camels zigzags a winding way up the mountain. The walk is long. The night is spectacular. We stop to rest, lean against the ancient rock and look into the enormous sky face. All the constellations I know and many I don't know; the swath of galaxies. Sometimes strings of 7 or 8 camels take up almost the whole path and force us to the side, kicking dust in our faces. My body aches. It's completely dark except for the brightest stars I've ever seen. We keep walking. An hour. Another hour. And another.

Now the steepest, rocky way to the summit. Over 1500 so-called steps from this point – just uneven pieces of stone, like a path of repentance, you just keep going, unable to look up or down, just one foot after the other, breathing – you and the mountain and the breath. This is waiting in motion. How much farther? Voices whisper "five more minutes, ten more minutes, we're almost there" to no one in particular. My legs are too tired to go on but I go on. I hear murmurs, a kind of quiet buzz and feel a sudden wind. We're here.

The morning star rising and the silver sliver of moon setting, rose light across the mountain tops layering out into the distance as far as I can see. The slowly spreading gift of light. Waiting. Waiting. When the first arc of sun crosses the horizon some people break into song—Greek? Arabic? Hebrew?—words I don't understand but the melody feels completely familiar. The red sun rises, the ritual spread-

ing back and forth across time, ah, the moment when the world trans-
forms from dark to light. We are always waiting in the circle of
changes. And the world is never totally in darkness.

—Susan Jackson
Mount Sinai

THE WAITING ROOM READER

Stories to Keep You Company

1
Mothers & Fathers

THE RED SWEATER

slides down onto my body, soft
lambs wool, what everybody
in school is wearing, and for me
to have it my mother worked twenty
hours at the fast-food joint.
The sweater fits like a lover,
sleeves snug, thin on the waist.
As I run my fingers through the knit,
I see my mother over the hot oil in the fryers
dipping a strainer full of stringed potatoes.
In a twenty-hour period my mother waits
on hundreds of customers: she pushes
each order under ninety seconds, slaps
the refried beans she mashed during prep time,
the lull before rush hour, onto steamed tortillas,
the room's pressing heat melting her makeup.
Every clean strand of weave becomes a question.
How many burritos can one make in a continuous day?
How many pounds of onions, lettuce and tomatoes
pass through the slicer? How do her wrists
sustain the scraping, lifting and flipping
of meat patties?   And twenty

hours are merely links
in the chain of days startlingly similar,
that begin in the blue morning with my mother
putting on her polyester uniform, which,
even when it's newly-washed, smells
of mashed beans and cooked ground beef.

Joseph O. Legaspi

FIRST GRADE

When Papa called from the street
I ran to the window.
He stood on the sidewalk
Holding his hat like a beggar.
Go tell Mama I need a handout!

I threw down three pennies.
He caught them, one at a time,
shuffled, bowed and hurried
off to the corner store
for the paper.

Five minutes later,
He rushed up the stairs
and whirled me around.
Are you set for school?
Yes, Papa, I can't wait.
What's that in the box?

And he gave me the gift—
a plaid bookbag with real
leather straps and my name
printed on the front in gold.
Inside: a yellow pad, a pencil
box, a sharpener that spewed
tiny curls of wood.

Papa put on his glasses
and turned to *The World*.
I sat on the floor
with a new sheet of paper
and began to practice my words.

Sondra Gash

WHITE
(an excerpt)

I don't remember the rooming house
my parents bought after Dad came home
from the war, or the day he climbed to the roof,
and while cleaning leaves from the gutter,
fell. I don't remember mornings Mom got up
before dawn and cooked for nine men,
or any of the chores she finished by noon –
backbreaking work which before the accident
took her and Dad all day. I don't remember
afternoons she dressed me in a little
red snowsuit, then took me by the hand
as we walked down the steep front steps
and crossed the street to Aunt Dee's. In fact,
I don't remember Aunt Dee, who watched me
while Mom caught the downtown bus
to Pearl Street, and ran Karmani's switchboard
trying to make ends meet
since Dad could no longer moonlight
driving drunks home in a cab.

What I do recall is someone – Aunt Dee? –
carrying me into a room,
putting me down.
White. I remember white.
White floor. White walls.
A lady. White dress. White shoes. A nurse?
I remember a bed. White sheets.
A tunnel of plaster.
I see my father's arm, as white
as this paper, sticking out
a hole in the plaster.
And as I watched him reach
under his pillow,
I see the smile on my father's face
as he watched me walk
toward the licorice stick he held
in his outstretched hand.

Christine Korfhage

ROSES

Whenever I try to dissolve
that man in anger
I picture him coming home
early from work in late May,
two quart containers of ale
bubbling foam in his fists.
Our mother says
Look Brad old Piney's protecting his roses
and we hold up our shirts
so he sees on our stomachs the gouges,
the dark glyphs of blood,
the lesson we learned from old Piney
who dragged from his brush pile
the harshest dead rose canes
and lashed them to our fence.
Then our father sets down his ale
and kicks open the door
and runs up the yard like a man
who never runs
and tears at the barricade of inch-thick canes
'til his hands become bloody dog jaws
and his yellow nylon shirt
is a butcher's shirt
and he heaves the canes
so they land on Piney's porch
and he stomps past us into the kitchen
and gets his ale
and escapes from us into his bedroom
where it's cooler
and stinks less of bleach and frying
and crying kids.
And then every room of the house
bursts with yellow roses
with cream and pink and white and russet roses
to carry to school in glass milk bottles
for the Virgin
and to bury our faces in
dizzy from that sweetness

Catherine Doty

AT BROTHERS DEPARTMENT STORE, DOWNTOWN

Aisles of cloches, lavender stockings,
ropes of crystal and pearl.
Our heels click on pink marble floors.
Wherever we turn, something new –
bakelite bracelets, marcasite rings,
rouge even for knees.
We dab our wrists:
Shalimar; Evening in Paris!

We could lose ourselves here, Mama says,
wrapping herself in a feather boa.
Is this too much? Do you want to rest?
I've had a long time to rest.
She takes my hand.
But we can have tea.

The Tulip Garden on the mezzanine –
deep leather banquettes, porcelain cups.
A few months ago she lay limp
on the bed, face to the wall.
Now she steps lightly onto the lift.
An usher in white suit
and gloves escorts us up.
Lingerie, Ladies' Apparel on 3!

Peach satin slips, lace pajamas,
a fringed sheath scooped low in the back.
This year prints are the rage,
the saleslady says.
Mama drapes a paisley shawl over her shoulders.
I try on a yellow silk dress.
We stare at ourselves in the beveled mirror.
You look beautiful, Mama.
You are beautiful, Faye.

Sondra Gash

RESHAPINGS
(an excerpt)

The shape of your womb
is how I learned to tilt my head
when listening hard, when taking in.
Your legs, one slightly shorter
than the other (not enough to limp
but enough to sculpt the muscles
of your back and tense your walk),
took me through my first merengue,
taught those small refinements
of sway and balance
and life spread over me
simply, cell by new cell,
as light spreads over a shadow,
lessons of pace,
lessons of patience.

                    *

A dream that you are talking.
You hold a peach and tell me
about the luxuries of shopgirls.
1943. Lord & Taylor, the lingerie
and nylon counter. Twenty,
no soldier to worry over yet plenty
to meet, the jewelry of the jitterbug
and free to stay in the city overnight.
You phrase it, the shiny black satin
of becoming a woman.

                    *

How quiet we are, the two of us.
Each reading in our favorite
chairs, the rainy afternoon
moving toward dusk and
the making of dinner.
I am proud to chop the onions
and peel the eggs.
I will earn a small piece of cake,
though not enough to ruin my appetite.
How the afternoon we made
enclosed us.

Howard Levy

ODE TO MY MOTHER'S HAIR
(an excerpt)

The provincial
river is transformed,
my mother
in a clear-sky afternoon
washes her hair,
dark as cuttlefish ink.

As a child
in the fringes of sleep,
when my fill of colostrum
swirled warmly inside me,
I often burrowed
my mole face
in my mother's hair,
the darkness beyond the banana grove.
I remember
how it brushed against my eyelids,
fending off the midnight dogs
of sleeplessness; tickled
my ears, deadening
the skeletons
of nightmares;
and how I breathed in
strands, which planted
the seed of the tree of memory.

My mother's hair is domestic hair:
absorbent to the scent
of her cooking –
milkfish, garlic, goat;
her fur of sweeping dust
clipped
in a bun, with wisps
that dangle
on her face, and dance
to floor scrubbing by coconut husk
to laundry five children soiled
to our endless pulling and shaking.

When my youngest sister
was born, our mother chopped
her hair, the incubating black hen
of her head ousted the starlings.
In hope of a reparation
for what we had driven her to do

I gathered locks
from her brush,
tied them with blue ribbon
and buried them in our backyard,
dusting the plot
with sugar and cocoa,
moistening the mound with honey –
all the goodness from the world of the living.
I believed
the earth resurrects
what is nourished in its belly.

And in this river,
my mother's wet, swirling hair
reminds me
of monsoon seasons
when our house,
besieged by wind and water,
teetered and threatened to split open,
exposing the diorama
of our barely protected lives
with my mother, seated, telling stories
to her children collected around her
while my sister and I are brushing her mane,
smelling of rose soap,
sprouting by candle light,
her hair which is always the other half of the world.

Joseph O. Legaspi

HOW TO FALL IN LOVE WITH YOUR FATHER

Put your hands beneath his armpits, bend your knees,
wait for the clasp of his thinning arms; the best lock
cheek to cheek. Move slow. Do not, right now,

recall the shapes he traced yesterday
on your back, moments before being wheeled to surgery.
Do not pretend the anxious calligraphy of touch
was sign beyond some unspeakable animal stammer. Do not

go back further into the landscape of silence you both
tended, with body and breath, until it nearly obscured all
but the genetic gravity between you.

And do not imagine wind now blowing that landscape
into a river which spills into a sea. Because it doesn't.
That's not this love poem. In this love poem
the son trains himself on the task at hand,
which is simple, which is, finally, the only task
he has ever had, which is lifting
the father to his feet.

Ross Gay

THE SOCKS

This pair once belonged to my father,
army green,

golden on the thinning
heels and toes, decades old –

they have disappeared into the dryer-netherworld
only to return repeatedly, wiser than before –

their elastics still grasp my lower calves.
When I slip into them,

I see my father in his footwear, like Mercury,
a copper-eyed young man, like myself,

brewing with stormy promise,
prepared to soar over the dusty world.

Dear socks, don't lead me astray.
Propel me from this dissatisfied life

to places where my father has never been.

Joseph O. Legaspi

FEDERICO FELLINI'S BIRTHDAY

Today, Mom, you would have been ninety and I
wonder what kind of old woman you
would have become because when you died
you were young.

I never knew til now that
you and Fellini shared
a birthday. You'd both be surprised
how the world's changed. Dad's okay.

His wife, who is younger than me by far, is
traveling soon to India and we, my husband
whom you barely knew and I, will stay
with Dad while she's away.

You'd be amazed how small
the world has become. There's so much
to say – I have grandchildren – for one.

If you could see Ruby Leah
named after you, you'd
die again, but this time
of happiness.

Karen Chase

2

Spouses & Soulmates

THIS CAN HAPPEN WHEN YOU'RE MARRIED

You find blue sheets the color of sky with
the feel of summer, they smell like clothes
drying on the line when you were small.
They feel unusual on your skin; you and your
husband sleep on them.

You find thick white towels that absorb
water. When you come from the bath, you are
cold for a moment, you think of snow for a moment,
you wrap yourself in a towel, dry off the water.

Now, you unpack your silver, after years, polish it,
set it in red quilted drawers your mother
lined for you when you were young.

You and your husband are in bed. The windows are open.
There is a smell from the lawn. It's dark and late. You
and your husband are in the sheets. He is like a horse.
You are like the grass he is grazing, you are his field. Or
he's a cow in a barn, licking his calf. It's raining out.

He gets up, walks to the other room. You listen
for his step, his breath. It is late. For moments
before you sleep, you hear him singing.

He comes to bed. He touches your face. He touches
your chin and lips. Later, he tells you this. He puts
his head on your breast. You are dreaming of Rousseau
now, paintings of girls and deserts and lions.

Karen Chase

THE DISHEVELED BED

The birds are back. I like to think
the first two, singing in the pines

four years ago, five floors below,
mated, gave birth, migrated, and came
back with their young, who also bred,

and whose descendants, and theirs,
now pair up and nest, a new generation
every year we've lived here, one extended
and extending family for the one

denied us, the random yet orderly
rise and fall of their songs rising as high
as our high-rise home, as you brush

out my hair and we straighten
together the disheveled bed.

Andrea Carter Brown

THE GIFT

In Japan long ago, when Koson
folded back the sleeves of his kimono,
picked up his pen and began drawing
the image that would later be carved
into cherrywood, then pressed
onto paper and colored in,
he had no idea that a century later
a man in rural New Hampshire
would unpin that print from his bedroom wall
where it had been hanging longer
than he could remember, roll and tie it
with curling red ribbon, then leave his home
in the dark, and drive past frozen fields and woods,
past farmhouses with wreath-covered doors
and candlelit windows, on and on,
to the roadside mailbox of a woman
he hadn't seen in over a year.
He just knew that as he moved that pen,
line by line, feather by feather, beak by beak,
loneliness drew two wild geese flying
before a moon so large it nearly filled
the page.

Christine Korfhage

MANGOES AND RAIN

We go over and over the same ground.
I worry about the plants,
the warmer than usual spring,
the frost and the fall and the winter
and we start again.

We go for walks on the first nice day.
You say, how lovely.
My heart is racing.
We read and lie next to one another.
Argue over money or sex.
My lip jammed suddenly against my teeth.
There's a spot of blood.
A sigh.
I think about the yard.
How I'd like it to be.
You buy a picture at some store.
You know I'll hate it.
Did I ever get a gift I wanted?
There is summer and I eat fruit you've brought.
Kiss you once in a while.
Turn away from your breath, wipe my hand across my mouth.

Come home.
Come home.
Bring me fruit, even if it's bruised.
Let's eat the same food every day.
Just do it here.

Jack Wiler

CATCHING MY BREATH

My body has learned many lies,
but here, in this bed we share,
they fall from me till I am clean,
a tree in winter,
awaiting the new season.

Richard Jeffrey Newman

BECAUSE

Because I refuse to learn to say goodbye,
these words – but because they are not my skin,
and because my fingers are not syllables,
and because your voice on the phone is not
breath I can take into my mouth and taste,
and the phone when we speak is not your body
in my arms or your hand lifting my chin
so our eyes meet when you say *I love you*,

and because when I imagine your hand
lifting my chin, I want to live within
that moment with you the way language
lives within us, I am here, wrestling these lines
into form, and because the form *is* me
when you read it, I'll be there, and we'll touch.

Richard Jeffrey Newman

THE BATH

I'd love one, she says,
and I draw the bath,
unbutton her blouse,
lay the tumble of clothes
on the bed and lift her up...

I thought I might never
hold her like this again,
her whole weight
in my arms, her fingers
wrapped around mine
as she sinks into the tub,
her nipples dark
in the silvery blue.

I set a towel on the ledge,
Morris, I'm sorry...she says,
Sha, I say, kneeling beside her,
squeezing the sponge,
spilling water down
the curve of her neck.

I feel her calm
as she leans back.
She's not dreaming now –
hair wet and curled
in the steamy heat,
arms raised over her head.

Sondra Gash

SOME TIME IN TRURO

I almost wake you.
It's not that you need to see the billowing
of the white muslin curtains, how they seem
another, more tender, quiet form of surf,
since making love through most of the night,
we billowed and curled
to and away from each other
in our own tides of want and rest.
And it is not because this is our first morning
ever entwined
and you need to see how the sky remains cloudless,
the sun draped along the ocean surface
and it's not that you need to see
that you sleep your effortless sleep
next to me.

I almost wake you
because I want a retelling,
how last evening, sitting on the beach,
the darkness falling around us like tapestries,
how this "might have been"
simply and finally began
in the gesture of an offered sweater.

I don't wake you
because you may be dreaming
and I may be in it,
and when you wake
you will slide your head onto my chest
and tell me your dream.
We will dive together into it
and match our strokes,
trim through the water and careless
of any destination.

Howard Levy

JAM

Our love is not the short
courtly kind but
upstream, down,
long inside – enjambed,
enjoined, conjoined, and
jammed, it's you, enkindler,
enlarger, jampacked man of many
stanzas, my enheartener – love
runs on from line to
you, from line to me and me
to you, from river to sea and sea to
land, hits a careless coast, meanders
way across the globe – land
ahoy! water ahoy! – love
with no end, my waters go
wherever you are, my stream
of consciousness.

Karen Chase

PRAISE FOR WASHING FEET

It was all I could have wanted of resurrection,
at that moment,
the fluid jug lifted to the basin, pouring
water so it landed with a sound like flutes
through the spruce trees, their cool
spacious gestures roused by wind.

You scooped the water in both hands
and splashed my two feet,
rounding, rinsing between toes,
the slow massage moving over
arches, heels, the soles
until we lay back in startled praise
for hands, and that cool water.

But today I come in almost too tired
to lift myself up the stairs,
know nothing at all to bring
what I need back to life,
unless it's our day of fluent hands,
the earthenware jug splashing
water like flutes; yet here I'm far away
and the only praise I know now
is to go again in some singular way
to a metal faucet and a small white basin
and let the abundant water flow
into my own two hands.

Susan Jackson

Daughters & Sons

BLUE

Blue hospital gown twists
and winds around me
as I turn from side to side,
moving toward the blue hour
of your birth; inside my belly you
swim past women with blue basins
on their hips going to the river to bathe,
past Mary Magdalene clasping her blue shawl
as she rushes into the cool blue Jerusalem morning,
you pass hills blue as the Serengeti at sunset,
your forefathers' blue sails lifting
in the wind as they head out to sea;
as you swim past blue starfish
in the reef shoals my temples pulse,
blue drums beat, I pant as I push you through the
blue currents of your ocean world into
light dazzling your new eyes child of the blue hour
air beating into your lungs till you cry out
the hymn of your arrival into the new homeland
you make for me in your coming.

Susan Jackson

HOME

I have a child.
She is my mother.
I lace my finger around
her little heel
and hoist her into the saddle.
Her quartz-tipped hand is my lead
as I show her the reservoir,
and the underpass where those
bundles sleep, swaddled and smelly.
We have no right here.
We must keep to the smooth path.
On her head is the velvet
cap I will teach her to tie
when the fat drops from her chin.
On her feet, patent leather
to slap and gravel and keep
time when I help her run.
I will not cry when we circle
the reservoir, skirting
those drooling babies under the bridge.
She will give me a home.
Daughter.

Celia Bland

THE DAY SHE GETS HER LICENSE

The car is as long as a city block
and sleek
the fins stretch out as far as the eye
can see
or so she imagines.
It's the early days
of metallic finish
the color of the car
blue frost or silver
depending on the way
light glints
off the surface
or how high
the sun is.
With the top down
the red leather seats shine
like the inside of a flower
like a flag in the wind
and her hair trails out
behind her, flying.
When the guy on the corner,
the cat with the long side-burns,
looks across the street
and whistles
she knows it's for her
she knows
she's beautiful
she will always be
beautiful.

Susan Jackson

MATTERS OF THE FLESH
(an excerpt)

alight

flesh of my flesh
you travel so fast
down the hall
down the hospital hall
your gown rushes out
like angel wings

angel

one hand wheeling your pole
tubes running out of you
through bags dripping
back into you

in another circulation
you were attached to me…
here is your second boy

you look awful

the new one quiet as a melon
sleeps flaunting a raspberry navel

while you my daughter run down the hall
keeping your first son's hand
espaliered to your side,
his apple eyes ripening in yours
(so dark and swollen from pushing)
to a quiet corner in the solarium…
talking with your two-year-old boy
giving him wrapped presents
from the new baby
his small back so very straight
as he listens to his new story
trying to size himself to the day.

together

I can see this love as though
it were matter, it rises as steam rises up
from deep hot springs

can you see it
there there oh there

     love

somewhere between the strawberry
jam on his finger
and his plastic bib of strawberries
a vapor surrounds you

     the spirit

weeping his visit over he must leave
his face breaks
with the weight of his new destiny
such a small boy his song
disappearing with the elevator

she is my matter
these are hers

     matter

through flesh
around flesh
holding onto flesh
coming through flesh
we are housed

Peggy Penn

EARLY MORNING SONG

In a fog this thick, I must count
on my fingers – eight days from you.
Everything has folded into fog,
as in Sung paintings
where the accidental details
of the world are lost
and the only clear thing
is The Way.

Each day here has grown hotter.
Yesterday afternoon, charred
by both heat and absence,
I sat still on the porch and tried
to write you a letter. Just too hot,
and someone came along who knew
a waterfall. The lesson is:
how often we get rescued.

I wrote once, as a son,
of fathers and sons,
silence as a medium of exchange,
loss compounded like interest,
the inevitable crash of laissez-faire,
but for you two asleep,
cradling your dreams,
I write something different:

true paths shine in the fog.

Howard Levy

THE DAY BEFORE HIS MARRIAGE

Folding his arms
at the water's edge,
his feet bury deeper
with every provocation
of the waves. Eyes are
skyward gathering blue,
I watch the water hit and miss us
with its jeweled light.
Small and laughing,
I hold him by the scruff
of his puppy neck,
and he runs toward the water
trying to catch it whole.

Later
when there was a stone on his heart, I could
feel it on mine as though a pendulum
swung between us, unmoved by time, and the arc
of separation narrowed to the time
his heartbeat lay under mine. He turns, I wave,
smiling from my distance as though to say,
what are you doing… just s t a n d i n g out there?
He smiles back, skips his stone expertly
across the water; dives after it and swims—
racing in his boy's crawl to manhood; now
sweetened with the certainty of what's beneath,
and what's above; certainty of lover
and of love.

Peggy Penn

FOR MY SON, ABOUT TO BE A FATHER

Making love last night with
my husband, not
your father, I thought how
sex is a lasting act.
I'm not talking about
genes, the long stream that
drips down from
one generation to
the next – we're all
in this together, it seems.

Karen Chase

PAUSE

A teenager now, already it's hard
for you to feel more than the practiced
ironies and diffidence, too many
hours already spent pretending
you've seen it all, and repeatedly.

An hour ago, I dropped a book
and it fell open to this – *only chance
can speak to us.* I thought of Picasso,
of how he found his sculpture of a bull
in the odd conjunctions of a rubbish heap,

an old bicycle seat lying near
a rusted handlebar becoming the bull's
head. I don't know if chance spoke
to Picasso, or why thinking of that
happy accident led me to the night

you were born. Your mother's water
had broken and, driven by worry,
the hospital two hours off, the road
fogged-in and narrowed to what
our car lights could dimly map,

I almost drove over a baby rabbit –
a distillate of rain and moon-shot fog
that formed suddenly out of mist,
and brought us to a standstill.
Your mother and I just sat there,

forgetting ourselves and where we were,
as slowly, and a little at a time,
the rabbit became solid and actual:
first the alert, twigged ears diamonded
by rain-lit mist at each hair's tip;

then the downy, crescent-shaped body
poised on those nimble-muscled feet
created for feints and dartings.
So vulnerable and yet so completely
at ease – only a rabbit, it took all

our attention. As we sat there,
we began to hear what was happening
around us – the sluice-rush of water

in a nearby brook and the fainter
background simmering of raindrops

in a fuchsia hedge touched by wind.
Even a dog barking and the ping
of rain on the car's metal roof
seemed a completely new language.
I can't explain why one incident

triggers another or why, together,
they become something else entirely.
I'd like to call it the plentitude of
the unintended. The truth is,
I don't know if chance speaks or if

the mind just cobbles together whatever
it needs – but this world is full of
accidental moments that can stop us
in our tracks and wake in us again
the strangeness we were born to.

Robert Cording

RUGELAH, 5 A.M.

The house is dark and breathing
deep under the covers.
I tiptoe to the kitchen,
lift bowls from the shelf,
mix cream cheese and butter.
Flour dusts my fingers
as I roll dough into a circle,
spread blackberry jam
with the back of a spoon
the way Mama taught me.
I work quickly, leaning over,
sprinkling nuts and raisins
on top, my hands
shaping ovals, folding,
crimping edges.

Light sifts through the windows
and I think of Mama, coming
home after so many months,
how we baked before dawn,
I, barefoot, she in nightgown
and slippers. Now I slide
the tray into the oven
and glide through the quiet
to wait for the raising.

Sondra Gash

AT THE HEART OF THINGS

I go through the simplest tasks
of the day lightened
as the Buddhist spirit of
mindfulness expresses itself
in folding clothes
one warm linen sleeve
lying against another
the cut grass
in full fragrance around me
as I gather peonies
for the table.
Their tall green stems
languish in the water
heads resting heavily
against the bowl's rim
as if under the weight
of a long remembered sorrow.

On the kitchen counter
basil for tonight's pesto
garlic and walnut's
sharp woody smell
still on the cutting board
the boiling water's steam
condenses on the window glass
and I realize how surely
these are nothing
compared to the abundant task
of gathering all this love.

Susan Jackson

THE SOUP

On the day of your scan I make a soup
to wean us from meat. Beans soak and blanch
an hour while I slit open the cell-
ophane wrap on the celery, chopping
the ribs into small pieces, the size
of the stones that follow an avalanche.
Carrots sliced into see-through orange mem-
branes, others hacked into jagged boulders, bi-
sected as though by the pressure of shift-
ing plates. Onions at knife point, suppurate
and toss themselves into the hot oil. What
is left? two blind see-no-evil potatoes.
Sweet herbs: I pull apart ovate leaves
of basil and sweet marjoram. Red kidney
beans slip out of their bladder skins, rubbing
against the Great Limas. Together,
they give off a kind of scum which keeps down
the foaming boil; instead it heaves and
swells, trembling like a bosom but does not
spill out. Thank God for scum! *I rinse my knife*,
watching its gleaming edge rotate under
the water; now there is only the wait.

Peggy Penn

POEM ABOUT FOOD

Loaves, fishes, desire, joy, eating,
eating, eating, 40 loaves, 40 fishes, eating,
drinking wine spodee o dee, drinking wine.
Saving the good for last.
The joy of drinking the last drop from the last jug.
The sopping of butter from the fishes.
The loaf crunchy and stale and hearty and what's in it?
How good could it taste with that wine we had last week at the wedding?
The last drop. Good.
The fish, was it haddock? Was it sturgeon? Was that roe on top? Was that
butter browned or compound?
The wine, the loaf, the fish, the bread crispy, not at all stale.
Perfect semolina even here in the desert and nowhere a mention of death,
just food, just wine, and food and dry turkey or dry wine or dry bread but
rich and glowing and needed.
Like if you had to eat.
Had to or you'd die.
You'd eat, you say but I say, you might not.
You might choose another way.
You might vomit or starve. I say, you might not eat.
I didn't, now I do.
Bread and wine and fishes.
Enough for a long time.

Jack Wiler

WATERMELON

1.

This morning, thirsty from the drain of night's sleep, I ate a thick slice of
sweet watermelon, cold, the kind of cold that could satisfy William Carlos
Williams. Forget the coffee, cream-cheesed bagel and bacon. I admit it:
I'm fixated with this fruit, green outside, red on the inside, like Christmas,
or my mother painted green, or like the Mexican flag without the eagle and
the stripes, but with seeds, which, when sun-dried and salted, become the
favorite snack food of Filipinos.

2.

I once told a tale to my younger sister of how I was conceived. Our moth-
er went out for a walk one fine day in April, maybe June, and she walked
down this path in the province, dried and brown and worn but teeming
with butterflies, and the withered leaves and splinters on the ground crack-
led under her feet, sounding like wet wood placed on a bonfire. She walked
until she stumbled upon a watermelon field where, overcome with thirst
and hunger, she picked the largest, fattest fruit, cracked it open with her
slender hand and found me in it. She carried me home and my true story
ended. My sister rolled her ten-year-old eyes at me and said, "Mommy had
sex with daddy."

3.

This summer night, I crave the satisfying sweetness of watermelon. I head
to the kitchen and open the refrigerator, searching, then remembering that
my father had eaten it for dinner: there is no more watermelon. All that
remains is a plum, burgundy, overripe, bitten, the teeth marks I know
belong to my sister.

Joseph O. Legaspi

RASPBERRY JAM

Breakfast shimmers.

Such a red, concentrated
essence of raspberry
so I see a clearing,
a butterfly
and those bushes, their berries
soft and scarlet as a cape of light.

I am near the point
where my joy explodes
into a profusion of breezes
each one redolent with fruit,
each one instructed
to find someone from my past
who was then or is now unhappy
and kiss them out of it.

Howard Levy

THE FRUIT STAND

When the last customer drove off
and Gram finally closed up and came in,
lugging baskets of bruised peaches and cherries
for tomorrow's batch of homemade pies,
usually all five of us cousins, sunburned,
lips stained from eating into the profits,
would be kneeling on chairs around the enameled
kitchen table, playing hockey with coins
from her cash box, impatient, waiting for her
to hook a fresh apron over her head,
give us scraps of dough, and a story,
Tell us the one about Grandpa.

Oh, you kids, she'd say. *Again?*
then look out the moth-covered window,
a tendril of honeysuckle dangling
from its upper right corner – too dark now
to see the battered old pickup.
How many mornings had she loaded it,
wedged screaming kids between ladders
and stacks of wooden crates, then started her rounds
up and down the rows of gnarled trees,
before backing up to the rotting platform –
the loading dock where he used to sit
and do nothing but smoke Lucky Strikes?

It was summer, she'd say. *Hot. Like this.*
No…worse. I was eighteen, working
at Huyck's Mill, binding wool blankets.
I must have been overcome by the heat.
Morris, somehow he got wind of it…

Then she'd stop.
And we'd eye each other, loving the pauses,
knowing she'd start leaning into the rolling pin,
her voice, exaggerated, deep, *Louise,*
I don't want to see you working like this.
Marry me. Marry me, Louise, or I'll throw
myself off the Hudson River Bridge.

And we'd be laughing, kneading our little mounds
of dough – conspirators, tilting back on the legs
of those chairs, not understanding completely,
but remembering how much he once scared us:
that one and only tooth – the way it stuck out

over his upper lip, and his voice
whenever he blew up at her,
Get those goddamned kids out of here!

And now, shoulders pulled up to our ears,
we'd clap our sticky mouths, powder them white
with flour dust, a little guilty perhaps,
but waiting for her to raise her eyes toward – what?
Heaven? The ceiling? That water-stained ceiling?
Her cue for us to join in, *I should've let him jump!*
I should've let him jump!

Christine Korfhage

TOMATO SANDWICHES

At the last moment it rained.
Though underage, we were allowed
to drive the station wagon into the overgrown
pasture. We stopped in the ferny asparagus bed
gone to seed. Rain tap-danced on the roof!
Across the windshield the wipers pulled
the water like curtains on a puppet show,
tucking us in.

Three sisters, we dined formally to start,
unwrapping the wax paper sheets, guided
by their neat hospital corners and folds.
But biting into the pillowy white bread
the mayonnaise oozed, and the lettuce
slipped away like hair tied with silk ribbon.
Next, the tomatoes squished and slid,
spattering our faces, our laps, the seats.
We were silly, then sillier as we pointed out
the boring carrot and celery sticks, the dull
boiled eggs, whose shells we resoundingly
cracked on our heads, laughing hard enough
we had to hold our sides. It hurt.

Chronic competitors, made wary for life
in the arms of parental approval, where else
would we find a checkpoint so lax, waving us
through to someone as close as a sister?

Georgianna Orsini

BRINGING HOME POTATOES

Lifting their rounded nubby bodies from the bag
moist and dirt grab the air.
They are not actually damp but still
speak the dark damp language
of underground, of earth
covering, touching them as they expand into it.

Could we have the same unstraining patience
growing eyes, waiting in the dark
unable to breathe in anything other than
this peculiar way of knowing that
everything is as it's supposed to be;
so sure of the inevitable harvest?

Susan Jackson

5
My Life, My Self

THE MATRESHKA DOLLS ON THE DRESSER

Hidden inside me
is a doll.
She looks exactly
like me
but she's smaller.
And hidden
inside her
is another.
Her cheeks
like mine
are ripe plums
and she too
wears a babushka.
We all fit
inside each other;
we're all
pear-shaped
little mothers.
At the center
we open,
except the last one,
the tiny one.
She's a seed
waiting.

Sondra Gash

IN THIS BIG BED

Somedays I don't even wash my face or brush my teeth. I love the
undisturbed
crustofsleep   that collects
in the corners
of my eyes,   remnants of the deep drape
that w r a p p e d my body
all night in my own bed   like the arms of
my Mother
—not her really,
but the broad Gesture of Mother
that each of us crave& keep   as icon
in the safe crib   of our hearts.

I don't even mind if you don't love me now.
I will again
tomorrow   perhaps, but not
this morning
with grace   spill ing the sun's e x cess over paper s & books
carelessly
strewn
on the bed   as if it
knows
they belong here
like a hip,   a   thigh,   a   wash   of   hair,   or a
fist   remembering
—a child's perhaps,
clutching mother's
forefinger   in that sign of   final   trust.

The mother that loves me deepest   sleeps beside me,   sleeps
inside
me
in this Big *B*ed.

Joan Cusack Handler

ANGELS

They're everywhere, baby-cheeked cherubs flying
On boutique signs, on cards and magazine covers,
In the serene sky of coffee table books.

They surround us like a halo that is no more
Than a suggestion, a dim waking to something
At the edge of our gaze when we look up.

Trees sway, a bird sings, propelling us to worship
Some source of warmth that will fill in the blank
Spaces of our hearts. Our angels never flash swords,

Flap their six monstrous wings like the sound of chariots,
Mete out judgments, or announce unexpectedly
A precocious child. They tell us to forgive ourselves

And love who we are; they focus us on abundance
So we may have enough for car and house payments,
The kids' tuition bills. They whisper – *there's a god*

Inside of you – and we believe. How good we feel
About ourselves, how unencumbered and free,
As if some transformation had surely taken place.

And so our days unravel in summer pastels,
The sun a mild version of itself, its trellised light
Nearly graspable, dappling the patio bricks and a table

Where a book is opened by the wind, a sign
Without meaning but beautiful, serving almost
No purpose at all except to create a kind of mild
Annunciatory sense that, yes, everything is about us.

Robert Cording

TODAY

I love the women in the deli:
two with handsome hands and doctored yellow hair.
They wrap my corned beef sandwich with crisp affection,
they give me extra mustard, extra napkins.
They remind me of the two blond girls in the country,
climbing their flatbed of sweet corn mid-July,
giving me thirteen ears instead of twelve,
giving me change: their sore little green-brown hands.
All steamed up, I carry my leaky lunch
to a rock in the park where I can't sit still to eat.
I could raise a child, I could save a person's life
or write a song. Each thought is thick as a fish
with connecting thoughts, every word needs
to be shouted and choreographed. I haven't slept
in three nights; soon I'll tip over, forget
that I'm swollen with God on days like these,
forget yellow food, bright day, flowered shelf paper,
dogs, radio, and the smells of cement and rain.

Catherine Doty

ON THE OLD ROAD

Once a thin line of horses came out of the night
and you thought you saw
wings close quietly at their sides
but then they disappeared back into the dark,
to the other side of the road
away from the car's headlights.

You are everywhere looking for a sign,
for the hand of God to lift you up like the sea
lifts the waves, everywhere looking
for something wonderful folded in the darkness
like a code you might cipher,
teasing out words that could teach you
to fix broken things, what makes light.
Just as you flavor tea with sage,
gather wild rosemary sprigs,
season lamb with coarse salt and garlic
you want to know how to be
like the rocks that rise up rounded
by so much water passed over them,
make sense of how we give ourselves to this world.
You're like anybody who asks for clouds,
who likes some white punctuation
to all that sky.

Susan Jackson

I LIKE SAYING NO

Pure No—straight from my source,
not diluted by *I'm sorry but*,
not tainted by white lies meant
to soften the blow or appease,
not shamed by the wish
Maybe she didn't hear it.
Genetically altered No
as indestructible as the roach.
Knife-edge No that cuts to the quick,
sticks in the hearer's craw,
rings in glass-shattering pitch,
flips things topsy-turvy.
Vitamin T No that inoculates
My self against intruders.

Teresa Carson

THIS LIFE

is a good life, a lucky
life in a Bar Harbor spring in
1999, where the sun
backs in the sliding glass doors and
three birds practice their solos
for the next millennium. I'm not
living in it, but this life is
good, a hand-thrown mug
of coffee tasting as thick
as the ashes of Troy, the faces
of women I've loved coming
back to this life, this good,
good life that lives in May
with birds, with a plump gray
cat sprawled in a sun patch
like the emperor of spring.
My God but it would be
a decent life to live the life
I live! I yearn for it sometimes
in dreams when I am far off
riding the shrunken boards of a ship,
thirsting for that one green spot
of the land that will be my home.

Christian Barter

THANK YOU

If you find yourself half naked
and barefoot in the frosty grass, hearing,
again, the earth's great, sonorous moan that says
you are the air of the now and gone, that says
all you love will turn to dust,
and will meet you there, do not
raise your fist. Do not raise
your small voice against it. And do not
take cover. Instead, curl your toes
into the grass, watch the cloud
ascending from your lips. Walk
through the garden's dormant splendor.
Say only, thank you.
Thank you.

Ross Gay

6
Everyday Miracles

PRAISE

I heard the dogs before
I opened the door late, after work –
first Maude who was dancing
in praise of my arrival for all she knew
it was: presence without end,
the end of waiting, the end
of boredom—
                    and then Li Po,
who, in the middle of his life,
learning to make his feelings known
as one who has carried breath
and heart close to the earth seven
times seven years, in praise
of silence and loneliness, climbed
howling, howling from his bed.

Laurie Lamon

ON A BEETHOVEN CELLO SONATA

I.

What would this cello be saying
if cellos could speak? But that
is a silly question; it is already
muttering behind, soaring over
in sudden realization, conversing
matter-of-factly with the piano,
which is clearly the timid one,
the one who makes excuses for his
outspoken friend, restates things
ironically, without emphasis, that we
might remember them as being
something less than the heartbreaking
visions of a mad soul. Listening
to this sonata, we may realize
that the thoughts we put into sentences
have no grip on us, take on
meaning only in long legato lines
that could have been made of anything, even
the scratching of a horse's hairs on his own guts.

II.

What I love about Beethoven is what
I so often hate about myself:
he never finishes anything. The strain
that labors cadence after cadence toward
resolution, wresting its course away
from the pestering piano, arrives
only after everything is so changed
that where it meant to go is no longer
possible, is there only as a memory
of where we might have rested. Perhaps
it isn't me, but life itself I hate
for this deception, though without it
(am I right about this?)
there is no beauty anywhere.

Christian Barter

PENTECOST IN LITTLE FALLS, NEW JERSEY

If I arrived early, I had to listen
To hundreds of sewing machines
Spiraling their high-pitched arias
Up against the mill's metal shell.

Each woman, a soloist withdrawn
Into her small cubical of work,
Sang the crazy hope of piecework—
Another zipper, another dollar.

A wall chart traced their numbers
In money's green line. It didn't
Record the pain when someone
Ran the needle through her finger.

I came at noon—between classes
At the state college where I read
Marx, and day-dreamed revolution—
To eat lunch with my grandmother.

Exactly at noon, there was a moment
Of quiet between the machines
Shutting down and the women rising
In common with their bag lunches.

They gathered at long metal tables.
High above them, a narrow strip
Of eave windows gave the only sign
Of weather and, sun, or gloom,

Let down a long flume of light
In which the women's bodies
Slowly relaxed, their lunches spread
Before them, and the patter of talk

Began in all those different tongues—
Haitian Creole, Canadian French,
Mexican and Puerto Rican Spanish,
Polish, Romanian, English,

Jamaican English—that spoke as one
The gospel of sacrifice and hard work.
They shared frayed photographs,
Smoked, spread the good news

Of children and grandchildren,
This one smart as a whip, this one
Taking dance lessons, this one a sight
To see hitting a baseball. There were

Some they worried about collectively,
And one who actually gave up booze
And became the man of their prayers.
Many more, of course, would not

Be saved no matter how hard
They worked. No end to the curses
And slammed doors, the hands
And faces bloodied by impotence

And rage. I often left the mill
Wondering if their hard ritual
Of work-eat-sleep-work ever changed
The state of daily lousiness at all.

The women believed, or had to
Believe. Over thirty years ago,
And still I see them returning to
Their machines, the unforgiving

Clock running once again,
The women bending to their work,
Losing themselves freely in that noisy
Oblivion because each of them

Cradles a secret happiness—that someone,
Working at his own sweet time,
Might tell the story many years later
Of how he had come to be saved.

Robert Cording

VESPERS

No one in church. The candles
know how to pray: they abandon themselves
in the silence until nothing's left
but the light they've become.

Joan Seliger Sidney

FLAMENCO NIGHT AT CENTRE CAP PÈREFITE

Lights like fireworks explode
anemone   aurora   coral.
The orderly beats life
into his guitar. He sings
to the woman who shrieks
when someone comes near.
She closes her eyes and smiles.

Maria rolls her chair
to the middle of the crowd,
swings back & forth,
then pops up on her wheels
to show her stuff.

And now Josette, blonde
hair cropped close, glitzy
earrings, beads and pin.
At her seat, like castanets
she claps her crutches.

Alone as always, the teenage
boy hides in the dark. Eyes
half-open, lost without therapies,
not a sound from his mouth.

In the middle of this night
I am swept onto the floor.
Hands on the edges
of my footrests swirl me—
I am not dizzy from the turns

My sea-green skirt
flares away my pain,
my shawl unfurls,
I throw open my arms
and spin, in my blood now
the music in the strings
of Juan's guitar, on the tip
of my tongue the song.

Joan Seliger Sidney

ODE TO ORDINARINESS

I.

Our little ration of things gone right, god of all that is
        Too humdrum for our notice, you carry out
Your work under our noses, predictable as the weather.
        When I open the door for today's paper,
There you are, unseen as always, in the manic circles
        Of a neighbor's setter that tosses a sunny
Cloud of goldfinches into the air and gives the giggles
        To a first grader two doors down, waiting
Inside this morning's teakettle mist and her father's coat
        Covering her shoulders. And now the sky
Is turning blue over the city and the yellow bus rolls up
        And the girl disappears in her seat, her father
Left waving to a window where the sun flares, suspended
        For a moment while he continues to shout
Last minute consolations for both of them: *I'll be waiting*
        In this same spot when you come back at three.

II.

And you're there with the mail, the usual bills and a letter
        From a friend (whose marriage fell apart
A year ago), who writes now about what stays the same:
        Still teaching and writing about X, playing
Some decent tennis; with a robin (what else) in the noonday
        Sun that scurries a few feet, stops, then tilts
Its head and holds steady in the great alertness and purpose
        Of its hunger. With the men eating lunch
Outside Linemaster Switch who soak up the good will
        Of this first warm day of spring and dream
Of getting in a little fishing in Maine. And you are in
        A conversation overheard at the supermarket –
Thank God the doctors caught it so soon—and in the face of
        The wife who knew that just this once,
And only for now, her husband had passed through the eye
        Of Fate's needle. Our little god of reprieves,
Of the breathing spaces between living and dying, between
        Disasters and raptures, you grant us the luxury
Of your dailiness, the *nothing much* we come to count on.

III.

We praise you: for the safe return of the school bus, for
        Everyone home for supper. Praise to recurrence
And status quo, to the sun returning like a second chance

After this evening's shower, and for sparks
Of rain igniting the rooftops of the Rogers Corporation
    Where chimney swifts that left with the sun
Have come back, soaring and banking now in the evening's
    Tints of yellow and orange. And praise for
The moon rising like a clockface and for the small triangle
    Of shadowed flesh where I've unbuttoned
My wife's blouse and for the identical feelings I first felt
    Leaning to kiss that exact spot twenty years
Ago. Praise for these last hours before sleep when we count
    Back through the day, and pick up a book
We've read over and over again because each time it is
    So familiar, so strangely different and new.

Robert Cording

WHY I DON'T DRIVE A NEW CAR

On the spring nights we drove them home
our first cars were beautiful:
sprung seats padded with greasy pillows,
chrome corroded, dings as endearing as freckles
and, when we leaned on the horns,
nasal bleats, foggy duck calls, or low and solemn farts.
We named our first cars:
Perdita, Joe Pickle, The Mermaid.
We had so many places we wanted to go.

Some mornings, when we weren't home
but waking up,
the sight of our cars from a second-story window
was all that we had to lash us to the earth.
When one of our cars was broken
our friends roamed the terrible cities
to find us in front of our houses, waving frantic,
and took us into their cars,
safe between their laundry and their lovers.

And what was as pretty as young, unbreakable bodies
tumbling from old Volkswagens at Sandy Hook?
And, if a parent died, what rich consolation
we felt at the sight of a dozen or so of us
spilling like clowns from a Day-Glo painted Valiant.
No, I don't need to be nagged to buckle my belt
in a voice as cold and fake as a Burger King milkshake.

Here's to a car that a pal can puke Southern Comfort in!
Here's to a car with a creamed corn can for a muffler!
Here's to the discontinued and disenfranchised,
longing for those parts no longer available.
I'll drive my rusting bones in a clamoring wreck,
a car like our first cars,
the cars that we loved
when we thought that we knew where it was
we wanted to go.

Catherine Doty

OUTBOARD

A drinking buddy gave our dad an outboard motor.
Dad kept it, up to its orange chin in bilge,
in an oil drum, up in the yard, and, after a few,
he'd go out and start it up, yelling, *Get back,*
you kids!—but we were already back, and ready to bolt
if the green plastic men we'd thrown in up and busted the thing.
But no tiny, acid-stripped skeletons churned to the surface;
the army remained at rest with the worms and the pear cores.
All that spring, when he felt good, he'd go watch his motor,
his nostrils straining to catch each oily fume,
a Chesterfield dropping ash down the front of his work shirt.
Once Shaky Louie, his pal, braved the terrible sunlight
to join him in motor watching, and, chatty by nature,
told us Dad had said soon that our freezer'd be so full of trout
there wouldn't be room left for even one skinny Popsicle.
By August we'd scrawled SS DAD on the slimy oil drum,
but he never noticed, just stood in the din, smoking, staring.
He never did lug that motor out of the oil drum—
he let winter do in the only toy he had, though it spat
muddy rainbows and roared like a locomotive,
and gave off the piercing and molten stink of hope.

Catherine Doty

WE'RE ALL GOING TO THE LAKE
(an excerpt)

We're going to the lake!
All of us.
We're loading up the minivans.
We're slapping up the kickstands.
We're running around the house,
screaming about how we can't
find our badges or our high band
or our favorite suit.
Which was right here and
we're getting up slow from lunch
and walking out to the car.
We're going to the lake!
Eight housewives, twenty five kids,
three lifeguards, one kid in the refreshment stand to dish up the water ice,
me and once in a while a dad and maybe some teenagers,
who are loud and look scary but
swim like shit once they hit the water
and smack!
What a lake to dive into!
A long brown ribbon of cedar water.
Trees brushing it's sides, bright blue skies
fill it with clouds
and turtles strung out on a log.
They're so tired from this hot, hot sun they forget to eat.
So the crappies and minnows
are all over the shallows.
Gotta get while the getting's good.
Far, far out on the lake a big bass leaps up, flops down
and nobody sees the water ripple out.
They're riding their bikes
down Jefferson or Monroe.
Towels over their shoulders
snapping in the rush.
A whine of spokes and muscle that's been going on for fifty years.
Fifty years of kids hauling their
bodies trawling streams of brown water,
small muscles stretched,
yelling, running, tight little balls that
cannon into the water!
O Joy! O headlong rush to water!
O the whir of spokes!
The shrieks!
We gotta go swimming!
Water calling water.
O Wenonah Lake!

Canoes, boats, rafts
big fat guy, belly up,
floating.
The only husband here today.
Me, watching housewives,
watching kids
splashing Dad,
slap of hand on water.
Ripples that go all the way to shore.
We're all at the lake!
We've brought everything we need.
Life jackets, blankets, sunscreen, towels, badges, bands,
balls, rubber killer whales, sunhats, sun glasses, coolers,
cocktails cleverly disguised as lemonade, water,
watches, buckets to carry water and
desire.
All for the lake!
On a hot, hot day.
We go to the lake for the water.
Come in!
Come in!
Come in!

Jack Wiler

7
The Earth

BOY

A great blue heron ambled along the creek.
At next glance, he was transformed
into a boy who strode out onto the road.

Perhaps like the Japanese Crane Maiden,
he was adopted by a couple, long childless,
like my husband and me.

This bird, just become a boy,
just bathed in bright water,
has come into a lather of sunlight.

Other children will sense his difference,
something of the heron, some memory of feathers.
Maybe the gray around his eyes will betray him.

When the curved finger of the new moon
beckons, if he survives into manhood,
he might translate the music

of birds, revealing its meanings.
He could make a song so true
and lucid, we will all be transformed.

Eloise Bruce

IF EVER THERE WAS ANYTHING TOO
BEAUTIFUL FOR THIS WORLD

If ever there was anything too big
and too beautiful for this world
it's my plumbago, a sprawling treeful
of cornflower blue trumpet
blossoms cascading everywhere.
Loves the light on this terrace
the way it takes right over, and must have
what the bees love – so many,
sweet flowers abuzz

this tree's like a woman
in a polka dot dress,
shimmers in the breeze
like a Marilyn Monroe with
too much color and too much glow,
she's a beacon, arms wide-
open to the sun and moon,
a dazzler all green and blue,
but she's a blaze spreading
everywhere, these branches,
they're exploding like fireworks,
takes your breath away

and she doesn't care,
sheds petals everywhere, makes a mess,
they stick in my hair, grab on my dress till
I'm blooming too, bemused and new
as anyone whose been touched
by who knows what
but everyone's asking
what happened to you?

Susan Jackson

THINKING ABOUT AUTUMN

I was looking at the garden
and thinking about autumn
and how I just can't like it
despite the colours of leaves
dahlias fat ripe elderberries
blackberries hips and haws
because it means winter's coming
and I don't like winter
despite how snow looks
on the trees I can see
from my kitchen window
frosty night stars
big fires and hot whiskeys
then I thought maybe I
should just learn
to content myself
because after all
it's the nature of things
and after winter there is
always spring and I love spring
the way may blossom is unbelievably
white and everything is bursting out
growing reaching moving
into lovely lovely summer
sun and bare skin
long light and short hot nights
then I saw the birds
lined up on the telephone lines
ready for leaving and I thought
screw contentment
if I had wings I'd go too.

Moyra Donaldson

WHAT I ALWAYS WAS

Though no maples grow on this block,
a maple tree's spinner sprouts inside the pot
the last tenant left out
on my Bronx apartment's fire escape.

Mornings, I've splashed the last of the stale water
from my teapot over it
until two leaves opened
to say their one clear green thing.

I thought I'd had enough of trees
when I unloaded my boxes here.
Restless twigs once blocked the light
from neighbors' windows and homecoming cars.

To punch an eye hole through the woods,
I placed my lantern on a stump.
Its light hardened the branches into rungs
that I climbed to the brightness from the city beyond our hills.

Moths pinned themselves to me like velvet hairbows
to bask in that glow. When they waddled over bark
or rust-pocketed leaves, they dissolved,
but on my sweatshirt's sleeve they became themselves,

legged, winged, and veined with clarity
of a drawing whose details develop against its frame's hard limits.
Each day in this city, I am becoming more and more like
what I always was.

Sherry Fairchok

REINCARNATION

As member of the Ailanthus clan
I'll stake my claim where other types of trees
refuse to grow – tenements, train tracks, cracks
in the Palisades, the used-to-be-full-for-three-shifts lot.
I won't care if my twigs are weak, my flowers
make some sneeze, my poisonous stems preclude
a food-chain spot. I'll take my place, with pride,
among beautiful-yet-unwanted common life:
gypsy moths, pigeons, thistles, feral cats.
When gardeners sneer *invasive pest* while cutting
down my trunk, I'll shrug and use their scorn
to feed my roots; so, even as they're gloating
good riddance to that trash, new suckers will
start breaking through their weed-free-but-dull ground.

Teresa Carson

GLORY

I'm out driving with my friends.
We're driving down US 1 from Russian River.
We've been to several wineries
and I've had six great wines
and several bad wines.
It's a beautiful day in a beautiful land.
The red wine I can't taste
because I've lost my sense of smell.
Then, at one winery, we're offered a Shiraz
That's so rich and deep,
it explodes in my nose and my mouth
and my head and I lean back and say
thank you.
Thank you for this wine,
for this day with my friends,
and then we leave.
So right here you'd think it all ends and
you'd be wrong.
Because right here it begins.
We drive down through the valley
and it's not all that impressive.
Then we wheel out to the coast
and God says,
take a look chump.
It's spread out all around.
Glory.
Like you'd never expect.
Sheer cliffs, sun glinting off beaches no one
should ever see.

Jack Wiler

AT THE END OF THE ROAD TOWARDS MONTAUK:
THE BLACK PINE

It's the only thing that survives out   here   where the s U n &   w *I* nd
scorch
everything
in sight.   These dunes are sacred;
                                        Sunday mornings, I should do my praying
                                          here.
                    Black Pine,   broad
                                         &deep:
            as any other   icon   I've lived by,
                                                    *PUSH*ed,   Bullied,
        tormentedby the *WIND*   while the SUN sits   High,
                                          harsh &   adoring.

                            I love how
                          this Tree,
                                      fists   thrOwn   out
                                 to defend it,
        Holds Its Ground,   like any Life   or Body
                          that knows
                              it's entitled.
                              & I love the twist of it
                  —the sometimes
                          u g l y
                            t
                               w
                            i
                               S
                            t—
        never bothered by beauty,
                          sculpting
                            its own body
                                from the   D a n c e
                of its   B A T T L E
                    WithThe   W *I* ND.

Joan Cusack Handler

85

MONTAUK AND THE WORLD REVEALED
THROUGH THE MAGIC OF NEW ORLEANS

In the afternoon, a jazz band
of thunderheads rolled in
playing "When the Saints"
so the ocean knew it was funeral
and commenced to lament and dance
and fan itself in the hot day,
the gulls too set to dancing
that quick step they are famous for
(and always do for the tourists)
and then the beach grass, never footloose,
began to clap out the rhythm
and shout
O this is some world
hot city, hot blooming

Howard Levy

SURVIVING HAS MADE ME CRAZY

I eat flowers now and birds follow me.
I open myself like an inlet
and dolphin energies
swim on through.

Wherever I go, I remain silent
and the silence begins to glow
till one eye in the light
outsees two in the dark.

When asked, I now hesitate
for there are so many ways
to love the earth.

I water things now constantly:
water the hearts of dead friends with light,
the sores of the living with anything warm,
water the skies with a thousand affections
and follow the voices of animals
into grasses that move like ocean.

I eat flowers now and birds come.
I eat care and things to love arrive.
I eat time and as I age
whatever I swallow grows timeless.

I eat and undie
and water my doubts
with silence
and birds come.

Mark Nepo

CavanKerry Book Titles and Authors

Christian Barter: *The Singers I Prefer*
Celia Bland: *Soft Box*
Andrea Carter Brown: *The Disheveled Bed*
Eloise Bruce: *Rattle*
Teresa Carson: *Elegy for the Floater*
Karen Chase: *Kazimierz Square, Bear*
Robert Cording: *Against Consolation, Common Life*
Moyra Donaldson: *Snakeskin Stilettos*
Catherine Doty: *Momentum*
Sondra Gash: *Silk Elegy*
Sherry Fairchok: *Palace of Ashes*
Ross Gay: *Against Which*
Joan Cusack Handler: *GlOrious*
Susan Jackson: *Through a Gate of Trees*
Christine Korfhage: *We Aren't Who We Are and this world isn't either*
Laurie Lamon: *Fork Without Hunger*
Joseph O. Legaspi: *Imago*
Howard Levy: *A Day This Lit*
Mark Nepo: *Surviving Has Made Me Crazy*
Richard Jeffrey Newman: *The Silence of Men*
Georgianna Orsini: *The Imperfect Lover*
Peggy Penn: *So Close*
Joan Seliger Sidney: *Body of Diminishing Motion*
Jack Wiler: *Fun Being Me*

Requests for copies of *The Reader* should be made by doctors or
hospital/medical facility personnel and addressed to:
joan@cavankerrypress.org
sgold@gold-foundation.org

or by mail

Joan Cusack Handler
CavanKerry Press
6 Horizon Rd #2901
Fort Lee, NJ 07024

Sandra O. Gold Ed.D.
The Gold Foundation
619 Palisade Ave.
Englewood Cliffs, NJ 07632

The Reader is available for purchase wherever books are sold.

Elegant Partnerships

Commitment to community is essential to CavanKerry's mission as a not-for-profit publisher. Dedicated to the written word and to outreach programs that bring the art of writing to diverse communities, CavanKerry partners with the Arnold P. Gold Foundation, dedicated to improving patient care, to extend this effort to include the medical and patient communities. The following programs are co-sponsored by CavanKerry and the Gold Foundation:

LaurelBooks: The Literature of Illness and Disability. These books focus on the lived experience of illness, specifically the intense emotional, physical and psychological effects on the patient and family. Illnesses explored in current *LaurelBooks* include: childhood leukemia, melanoma, bone marrow transplant, multiple sclerosis, suicide, sexual abuse and schizophrenia.

In Their Own Words: Patients Speak is an innovative program that targets medical schools across the country. Recognized as valuable clinical tools, free copies of *LaurelBooks* are provided to participants, and visiting authors meet with medical students and other healthcare practitioners for readings and discussions. The books and all expenses are gifted by CKP and Gold.

The Waiting Room Reader: Stories to Keep You Company is part of CavanKerry's *GiftBooks* outreach initiative which offers free books to underserved communities and is an extension of our *LaurelBooks: Literature of Illness and Disability* imprint. *The Reader* is offered free of charge to underfunded hospitals and medical facilities to make available to their patients, their families and loved ones. Several thousand copies of this first edition have already been gifted thanks to the generosity of another CavanKerry partner, the Liana Foundation.

Both CavanKerry and the Gold Foundation are deeply grateful to Liana for making it possible for us to launch this venture and give life to the dream. The patients are too grateful; their response has been overwhelmingly positive. It is our shared hope that funding will become available for us to distribute *The Reader* to thousands of doctors', clinic and hospital waiting rooms nationwide. To help us support

this ambitious mission and to expand the reach of *The Reader* beyond
the medical arena, we are now offering it for sale wherever books are
sold. Our long range dream includes bi-lingual and large print ver-
sions as well as the creation and publication of subsequent editions of
The Reader every 3 to 4 years.

www.cavankerrypress.org
www.humanism-in-medicine.org

Inquiries or requests from interested individuals or agencies regard-
ing any of these programs are welcomed. Contact Joan Cusack Han-
dler at joan@cavankerrypress.org.

Your Words & Stories

Feel free to record your own stories or comments here and share them with other patients who pick up this book.